SUGAR FIGHTER

SUGAR DADDIES BOOK #1

CHARITY PARKERSON

--Warning: This book is intended for readers over the age of 18.

Copyright © 2018 Charity Parkerson
Editor: Hercules Editing and Consultants
ISBN: 978-1-946099-33-4

INTRODUCTION

ZEKE IS THE OLDER MAN. THE RICHER MAN. THE MAN WHO PLANS TO GIVE KOREY THE WORLD.

As MMA's Light Heavyweight champion, Zeke's million-dollar matches and multi-million-dollar sponsorships have given him the freedom to do whatever he likes. It pleases him to spoil Korey. Before Zeke's best friend Charlie was deployed two years ago, he made Zeke swear he'd care for his brother Korey if anything happened to him. When Charlie is killed by a roadside bomb, Zeke takes the young college student in, determined to give him everything he requires to succeed. He never expects to end up hoping he can keep Korey under more than his roof. He needs Korey beneath him.

If Korey had been in his right mind after Charlie's death, he would've turned down Zeke's offer. By the time he realizes his mistake, he's already addicted to Zeke's powerful presence. He never meant to end up dependent on the man's smiles and hot glances. The money, Korey could live without. The man has him hooked. There's only one problem —neither man wants to cross the line from friends to lovers, ruining what they have.

Sugar Fighter is a short introduction to a new series by Charity Parkerson, Sugar Daddies. This series will feature male/male May/December romances where the men are hot, rich, naughty, and don't like to be told no.

ONE

SWEAT GLISTENED ON ZEKE'S SKIN. A BEAD rolled down his back. Korey's mouth watered. This was Korey's favorite time of day. It was supposed to be his study time. In a way, it was, except instead of cramming for his next exam, Korey memorized every inch of Zeke's body. A snort escaped him. Luckily, the sound of Zeke's fists, knees, and feet hitting the punching bag drowned out the noise. Korey already knew every detail of Zeke's body. He could probably sketch the man from memory alone. In the dark. Blindfolded. Zeke was Korey's roommate. Well, roommate might be a stretch, considering Zeke had millions while Korey was broke as shit. Still, they lived together. Korey chose not to dwell on the semantics of their arrangement.

Each day, after his final class, Korey came here to

catch a ride home with Zeke. He had a car, but if he chose to use it, he would miss this. Every day, Korey sat in the same spot, book in hand and longing for what he could never have. Zeke Armstrong was the Light Heavyweight MMA champion. He had fourteen years on Korey, more money than Korey could ever dream of having, and no obvious interest in anything beyond fighting. Korey was nobody. He was a college student whose brother found him a place stay in a state where he knew no one. Living with Zeke was heaven and hell. Korey wanted him. It would never happen. Zeke's hard muscles bunched and rolled with each move he made. Korey caught himself keeping time with Zeke's blows. *Punch. One. Two. Kick. Three. Four. Knees. Five. Six. Reverse.*

Zeke turned, catching him staring. Light blue eyes flashed with good humor. Korey's stomach muscles clenched with desire at the sight. Zeke's sexy lips turned up in one corner. "Aren't you supposed to be studying?"

Korey swallowed past the lust crushing his windpipe. "Don't worry. I'm still acing everything."

"Damn right, you are," Zeke said, wiping the sweat from his forehead. "I expect it to stay that way." Zeke motioned a tape-wrapped hand Korey's way as he switched his focus to his usual sparring partner, Maverick, who was working out nearby. "This kid will cure cancer someday."

Heat crawled up Korey's cheeks. This was another reason he couldn't stop fantasizing about Zeke. The man was freaking amazing. On the outside, Zeke was perfection. He was six-foot-four-inches of two-hundred-pound muscle. Blond hair and blue eyes with deep lines at the corners of his mouth when he smiled. Korey swore angels sighed when Zeke laughed. But, on the inside, Zeke was a million times all that. When Korey moved to California from Alabama to get his medical degree from Stanford, he'd known he was headed for the unknown. His original plan had been to live with his oldest brother, Charlie, who was a marine stationed in Palo Alto. Two weeks after Korey started school, Charlie was unexpectedly deployed. Three months later, Charlie had been killed by a roadside bomb. Zeke had shown up, said he'd promised to take care of Korey if anything happened to Charlie. Two years later, Zeke still kept that vow while never once making Korey feel unwelcome or like a leech. Of course, Korey fully intended to make it all up to Zeke someday. That was why he never gave less than his all. Korey owed the man everything.

"You'll need that medical degree if you keep hanging out with this guy," Maverick said, pulling Korey's focus his way. "An old man fighting past his prime needs a good doctor in his corner," Maverick said, laughing as he pretended to hit Zeke in the ribs.

Korey's embarrassment fled. "Really? Who do you have lined up?"

Maverick threw his head back and roared with laughter.

Zeke tossed him a wink. "Let me grab my stuff and we'll head home."

Korey nodded and focused on packing up his bag. He eyes needed something else to do other than watching Zeke walk away. Korey already worried his lust couldn't be hidden any longer.

Maverick claimed the empty chair at Korey's side. "Are you coming to Vegas with Zeke this weekend for his match?"

"I'm not sure," Korey said, shoving his book in his bag. "We haven't talked about it." That sounded better than admitting Zeke hadn't invited him.

"You should go with me."

Korey froze halfway through zipping his backpack. Maverick wasn't a bad-looking guy. His dark, perfectly styled hair, honey-colored eyes, and cut body were downright amazing. In fact, most people would probably kill for that invitation, but Korey wasn't sure how to take it. Korey didn't hide the fact he was gay, but he didn't exactly flaunt it inside a fight club filled with straight guys.

Korey kept his gaze locked on his hands as he finished zipping his bag. "Um. How do you mean?"

Maverick's tone changed when he answered, turning sultry. "I thought I could pick you up," Maverick said, leaving no room for doubt of his intentions. "We could see the town afterward and you could stay with me."

Wow. Korey didn't know what to say. Not only was he caught off guard, Maverick wasn't Zeke. It was funny how Korey's heart refused to give up the dream of Zeke, even when an equally amazing offer presented itself.

"Or we could skip seeing the town," Maverick said, amending his offer. "And you could just stay with me."

"The hell you say," Zeke growled, appearing over Maverick's shoulder. His expression was thunderous. Korey had never seen the man angry before. He was now. There was a line between Zeke's eyes, and they flashed with barely suppressed rage. "Korey isn't ruining his life by getting mixed up with any of the no-good fuckers in this building."

Maverick's usual good humor never slipped, not even beneath Zeke's obvious fury. "Damn, Zeke. Tell me how you really feel. You should let the boy come out to play for at least one weekend."

Korey couldn't stop switching his gaze between the two. He'd never heard Zeke give anything but praise for his fight family.

Zeke didn't take Maverick's bait. "Let's go, Korey."

Korey stood, intent on following Zeke to the door.

Maverick grabbed his hand before he could get away. "Think about my offer. Here's my number." A scrap of paper appeared in the man's free hand. Korey reached for it. Maverick's thumb brushed Korey's wrist. An unexpected spark traveled up Korey's arm at the move. "Let me know."

"Let's go, Korey," Zeke called without looking back.

Korey's gaze moved between Zeke and Maverick. Maybe he would go. It was obvious Zeke thought Korey would level his life for a man. Korey wasn't that stupid, but it was nice to be wanted. Zeke would never want him. Eventually, Korey would have to accept it.

WITH HIS GAZE locked on the road, Zeke raged.
Fucking Maverick. He couldn't believe that dick's
nerve. For two years, Korey had been showing up at
Powerhouse Training after class. Everyone knew
Korey belonged to him. Maybe "belonged" went too
far, but the guys sure as fuck knew Korey was off
limits. They didn't mess with him, look at him, and
they damn sure didn't try to hook up with him. The
problem was Korey was too pretty for his own good.
His dark hair was always perfectly styled. The dude
just looked like he put time in on his appearance. It
didn't help the guy had unusual gray eyes framed by
long, dark lashes and perfect skin. He looked like a
goddamn angel. Except for Korey's lips. Those were
made for sin. Zeke mentally swiped a hand over his
thoughts, wiping them away. Korey was too young
for the ideas he gave men. Fuck. He was too young
for the way Zeke wanted him.

"Are you okay?"

Zeke tore his gaze away from the road long
enough to glance Korey's way. "Yeah. Why?"

Korey shrugged. "I don't know. Your jaw is
flexing like you're pissed."

The worry in Korey's tone had Zeke counting to ten in his head. It wasn't Korey's fault he turned Zeke into a perv. If Charlie was still alive, he'd rightfully kick Zeke's ass for the impure thoughts he had every second of the day about Korey. "I'm good. Just mentally preparing for the fight this weekend, I guess." He flashed Korey a smile, hoping it didn't look half as feral as it felt. "Sorry. What do you want for dinner?"

Korey didn't respond right away. When he finally spoke, his voice came out stilted, as if he worried he might say the wrong thing and set Zeke off again. "Would you tell me? If something was wrong, that is."

"Sure." The lie rolled so damn easily from Zeke's tongue it surprised even him.

"Okay."

A long, loud litany of cursing rang out in Zeke's head. Korey sounded sad. "We could order pizza," he offered, hoping to lighten the mood.

"You can't have pizza for three more days." The laughter in Korey's voice had the pressure easing in Zeke's chest. "I'll make a deal with you, though. If you win, I'll buy you the biggest pizza New York's Second Home Pizzas sells."

At the mention of Zeke's favorite pizza place,

Zeke's mood lightened even more. Korey knew him better than anyone. That was one of the reasons Zeke couldn't understand how Korey hadn't realized Zeke would trade everything he owned if Korey would act on the way he stared at him. Every day, Korey watched him train. Each day, it got a little harder to ignore the way the man's gaze stroked his skin. It was addictive. No one made him feel as powerful. He needed to make Korey feel at least one-quarter of the happiness he did.

"Did you want to go to Vegas with me? I hadn't asked because I thought maybe you'd have better things to do than being stuck with me while I do all the pre-match shit they require."

Korey didn't answer right away. When he responded, he spoke slowly, as if measuring each word. "I'd love to go if you want me there, and you're not just asking because you don't want me there with Maverick. Obviously, I don't really know the guy, and you do, so I'm sure you have your reasons." Korey released a low growl. The sound stirred Zeke's cock. "I don't know what I'm trying to say. It's like you said, you'll be busy with interviews and weigh-ins. If you don't want me underfoot, I don't want you to feel obligated to bring me along. You already do way too much for me."

Zeke knew Korey was uncomfortable with how dependent he was on Zeke. The thing was, it was all intentional on Zeke's part. He'd purposely overtaken Korey's life. Korey was the only person Zeke couldn't live without. Since he couldn't say that, he went with an alternative truth. "You're my best friend, Korey. There's never a moment I don't want you around. I know you like going to my matches, but I don't like making you feel obligated to be with me every time. It's my job."

A soft, sexy laugh came from Korey's side of the car, punching Zeke in the chest. "Now that we've established we're not obligated to each other, I'd love to go with you."

Without thought, Zeke reached over and linked fingers with Korey. It wasn't the first time they'd held hands. By nature, Zeke was a sensory driven person. He caught himself touching Korey more often than not. Korey accepted it, never seeming to take it to heart. The more Korey let him get away with, the more Zeke took. He imagined, one day soon, Korey would find himself tied to Zeke for life with no clue how it happened. Zeke would know. He planned it that way.

Even though Zeke had a large house, it wasn't big enough to share with Korey. There was no place he went where the man's presence didn't show itself. Of course, Zeke never tried getting away from him. If Korey made dinner, Zeke helped. If he studied, Zeke quizzed him. Chances were good, if they'd met under different circumstances, Zeke would've fucked the guy and never looked back. Instead, he fantasized but never touched. Lust had warped and transformed until Zeke had woken up one day completely owned by Korey.

"Do you want me to heat up one of these meal prep things while you shower?"

Zeke lifted his arm and pretended to sniff. "Are you saying I stink?"

Korey's face remained blank, keeping his thoughts hidden. "Yes. I'm saying you stink."

Zeke knew Korey was joking. Korey would never say such a thing and mean it. He was too nice, which meant Korey was in the mood to tease. Zeke was his man. "I smell like cotton candy, babies, and chocolate. You're the ripe one around here."

A smile stretched Korey's lips, stealing Zeke's breath. The man's dimples were hot as hell. "Babies?"

Zeke turned the water on in the sink. "You heard me. Babies—like baby powder and youth. You smell like a teenager's bedroom. I'll fix it," Zeke said, pulling the spray nozzle from the sink, and spraying Korey's chest.

"Ah, man," Korey yelled. "Is that how this is going down?" Korey grabbed a nearby half-filled glass of water leftover from that morning and tossed the contents in Zeke's direction before Zeke could jump out of the way. His pants took the brunt of it.

Zeke tossed the nozzle toward the sink and held his hands up. "Okay. Truce." He knew from experience they could destroy a room in no time and they'd have to clean up their mess. Korey's laughter made all water damage worthwhile.

"Truce," Korey agreed as he lifted his shirt up and over his head. Zeke ate the man alive with his gaze while Korey used the shirt to dry his face. Korey wasn't exactly the opposite of what usually attracted Zeke, but he also wasn't Zeke's normal type. In the past, Zeke had only dated men with similar interests. Guys who lived for the gym. Korey had a runner's body—slim and tight but not muscular. Zeke had never found anyone sexier. While distracted by all the fantasies of what he could do to that body, Korey caught him off guard, snapping him with the shirt. He got a second shot in before Zeke snagged the shirt. A tug of war began, each refusing to give up their hold until their chests met. Zeke went hard.

There was no slow stirring of desire. The instant their skin met, Zeke was on fire. Images of bending Korey over the counter and fucking him hard filled Zeke's head. Korey's smile fell. His gaze dropped to Zeke's mouth. A flush touched his cheeks. Zeke shifted even closer. Korey leaned in. For a moment, they stood with their mouths an inch away from touching. Korey's breaths fanned across Zeke's face. His eyes fell closed. Zeke quickly stepped back. Reality crashed down on him. This was Charlie's baby brother. He'd trusted Zeke to take care of him. Not use him as his live-in whore.

"I need a shower." Without a backward glance, Zeke headed for his room. He needed release before he fell on Korey with his dick out.

KOREY WATCHED ZEKE WALK AWAY. His muscles tensed as he fought the urge to chase after him. Sometimes, Korey thought he saw something in Zeke's eyes. Those moments kept Korey hanging on when he should've found someone else long ago. His body ached. He felt empty without Zeke inside him. His lips tingled with the need to be kissed.

Unquenched desire made him almost insane. Before Zeke, Korey hadn't known a person could die a little every day from loving and craving someone unrequited. When they'd gotten home, he'd been starving. Now Korey felt sick.

He headed for the shower. No amount of food would fill the ache in his gut. While waiting for the water to heat, Korey stripped. His reflection held him captive. He didn't lack in confidence. If Zeke had been someone else, Korey might have thought he stood a chance. Unfortunately, Korey didn't look like any of the men who worked out at Zeke's gym. He couldn't compete. The image of how Zeke had looked at him in the kitchen flared to life in Korey's mind. He touched his lips. His eyes fell closed. Without thought, his hand slid lower. In his mind, it was Zeke's hand traveling his skin. Korey's breath stuttered from his lungs as his fingers encircled his cock. He let the lust overtake him. Fantasies filled his head. If Zeke ever gave him a chance, Korey wouldn't know where to start. A thousand times he'd been on his knees for Zeke in his mind. Countless nights, Zeke's hard cock filled Korey's ass in his dreams. Chances were better than not they'd never be together. That knowledge didn't stop Korey from stroking his dick with Zeke's name on his lips.

His lips parted on a pant. His skin tightened. Korey gripped the bathroom counter with his free hand when his knees threatened to give. In his mind, he held Zeke's headboard while straddling the man's face. Zeke licked his balls and asshole. He let Korey ride his lips. The man's skilled tongue and willing throat sucked him closer to the edge. Loud gasps reverberated off the walls of the bathroom, getting lost in the sound of the water beating the floor of the shower. Korey's hips moved against his tight fist. He fucked his hand. The tightening of his balls became a pressure in his shaft that beat against his crown. Korey's lungs stopped. The world held its breath. Sound disappeared. His gaze met Zeke's behind his closed lids. Ecstasy slammed into Korey, forcing him to swallow a cry. Jet after jet of semen coated the sink. Korey didn't stop pumping until every spasm of pleasure stopped, leaving him spent.

His eyes opened. Korey stared at his reflection. He looked every bit as wrecked as he felt. A familiar fear landed on Korey's shoulders weighing him down. It was only a matter of time before Korey broke, and he admitted his love for Zeke. What would happen when that day came? Korey could live with any outcome, except Zeke's hatred or his pity.

KOREY WAS IN HIS CHAIR. Zeke bit back a smile. Shortly after Korey moved in, he'd taken a liking to Zeke's recliner. The first time Zeke busted Korey sitting in his chair, he'd pulled the man to his feet, reclaimed his seat, and dragged the man into his lap. He'd let Korey know right then the only way he'd get Zeke's chair was by sharing it with Zeke. That night started a new trend—Korey relaxing in his lap. Korey read. Zeke watched TV and tried his damnedest to hide his constant erection. It was a balancing act.

As Zeke cleared the door, Korey stood. His gaze never wavered from the book in his hand as Zeke sat. Without missing a beat, he crawled into Zeke's lap and kept reading. Unlike usual, Zeke didn't bother turning on the TV. Instead, he wrapped his arms around Korey and held on. It never failed to amaze him how Korey could tune out the world while reading, leaving Zeke free to stare at him. Tonight, he needed to hold Korey. It wasn't that Zeke didn't know Korey would eventually meet someone his age and leave Zeke behind. Maverick's invitation to Vegas brought all Zeke's worst fears to life. There was nothing wrong with Maverick. He was closer to Korey in age. The guy had a good job, working as a firefighter. In fact, if things were different, and Zeke had to choose, Maverick would be the man he'd pick for Korey. But things weren't different because Zeke couldn't escape the truth. He was in love with Korey.

Zeke kicked out the footstool and leaned back in the recliner. Korey settled against his chest and kept reading. Without thought, Zeke skimmed his fingertips down the back of Korey's arm. When he realized what he'd done, he forced his hand still. Korey was shirtless, wearing nothing more than thin pajama pants. Chill bumps rose on Korey's skin. Zeke snagged a nearby throw blanket and covered them. He had no clue how much time passed before the book slipped from Korey's fingers. Zeke grabbed it and set it aside. His hold tightened on Korey. Korey shifted in his sleep, cuddling against Zeke's chest. His chin tilted upward, giving Zeke the freedom to stare openly at the man's sexy face.

Those gorgeous lips called to Zeke. His hand lifted. He couldn't fight the temptation. He skimmed Korey's bottom lip with his thumb. It was as soft as it looked. Zeke held the man's chin. With his thumb still pressed to Korey's lips, Zeke lowered his head and pressed his lips to Korey's forehead. With the man's scent filling his nose and his lips pressed to Korey's skin, Zeke got to pretend for a second that Korey belonged to him.

Korey shifted in his sleep again. His face moved higher, as if he silently begged for Zeke's kiss. The desire eating at Zeke's gut all hours of the day took control of his mind. He could no more have stopped himself from kissing Korey than he could stop time from moving. When their lips touched, even the air seemed to hold its breath. Korey pulled away. Zeke's hand wouldn't stop stroking Korey's face—like it had a mind of its own. Korey was awake now. He held Zeke's stare. His gaze moved over Zeke's face, searching. Zeke held his breath. He couldn't explain. Korey shot forward and opened his mouth over Zeke's. Zeke had craved Korey for too long. He couldn't push the man away. Korey's tongue touched the corner of Zeke's mouth. Zeke opened for him. As their tongues brushed for the first time, Zeke went hard. Jacking off in the shower with Korey's name on his lips didn't save him with Korey's body against his, and the man's tongue filling his mouth.

Korey changed positions, deepening their kiss. The move also had the man's erection poking him in the stomach. Goosebumps skirted across his skin. His muscles clenched. Zeke's hands massaged every part of Korey he could reach. Korey bit Zeke's bottom lip. Zeke's palm collided with Korey's cock—skin on skin, making him realize he'd shoved his hand inside the man's pants. His fingers automatically curled around Korey's dick. The way Korey gasped against Zeke's mouth had Zeke doing everything in his power to drag more sexy sounds from the man in his arms. He massaged Korey's cock. Korey moved against his hand, sucking Zeke's tongue and holding on to Zeke's shoulders in a death grip. There was no going back. Zeke already knew he'd hate himself later. Right now, he didn't give a damn about anything except making Korey see stars.

A moan vibrated around Zeke's tongue. Zeke doubled his efforts, stroking faster. His dick twitched and leaked inside his underwear as if the pleasure was his own. Korey's breathing turned ragged. He tore his mouth away, obviously incapable of catching his breath while poised on the edge of release and kissing Zeke. With his head thrown back, gasping for air, and openly fucking Zeke's fist, Korey was the sexiest fucking sight Zeke had ever seen. Zeke's eyes burned with the need to blink. He couldn't miss a second of watching Korey in the throes of pleasure. A cry escaped Korey as hot cum hit Zeke's chest. Air sawed in and out of Zeke's lungs as if he'd run a marathon. Zeke ached with the need to get inside Korey. He didn't stop pumping Korey's cock until Korey recaptured his lips. Zeke hugged Korey close, uncaring of the mess between them.

"Korey," Zeke breathed between kisses. "I can't stop." He'd wanted this man too long. "You have to make me stop."

"I don't want to," Korey said, changing angles and going deep.

Zeke's last thread of resistance snapped. He pushed to his feet, holding Korey. Korey wrapped his legs around Zeke's waist, holding on and still trying to kiss Zeke as Zeke headed for the bedroom. He already knew. There was already a voice in the back of his mind, whispering this was a mistake. They'd passed the point of return. Korey bit his shoulder. Zeke almost didn't make it to the bed. Never in his life had he needed anyone like the way he required Korey for his existence. He tossed Korey onto the mattress with more force than necessary. He tore at their clothes before digging through the bedside table for lube and condoms. When his weight came down on Korey, Korey's body arched against him, as if the man had waited his entire life for Zeke's nude body to touch his.

Zeke stared down at Korey as he suited up and

swiped lube over Korey's asshole. The flush on Korey's cheeks and the way he chewed at his kiss-swollen lips was the sexiest sight Zeke had ever seen. He painted the perfect picture of turned-on male. It was as if his cum didn't already stain Zeke's balled up shirt in the corner. If it was anyone other than Korey beneath him, Zeke would have the man's face pressed into the mattress already, but it wasn't. This was the man he wanted. He needed to see Korey's face when he took him. He dragged Korey's body closer and swiped his crown across Korey's asshole, teasing them both. Zeke braced his hand on the headboard, leaning in.

Korey pressed his palm to Zeke's stomach, stopping him. "Go slow."

With two words, Korey calmed the storm raging inside Zeke. The need clawing at his skin, threatening to rip him to shreds, transformed. If Korey had been with anyone in the past two years, Zeke hadn't seen it. Hell, it was possible Korey had never been with anyone. Instead of putting him off, the thought only stoked Zeke's possessiveness. He shifted positions and captured Korey's lips before pushing past the tight ring of muscles surrounding Korey's asshole. He didn't thrust deep. Zeke slipped inside an inch and froze. His tongue toyed with

Korey's as he gave the man time to adjust. Zeke had known Korey's kiss would be amazing. It was so much better than all his fantasies. Zeke rocked another inch deeper. Sweat broke out on his skin. He hoped he didn't explode before he was fully seated. Korey was so hot and tight.

"Zeke," Korey whispered against his lips, snapping Zeke's mind.

He thrust, going deep, and ripping a moan from Korey. Zeke tried going slow. Korey was too perfect in every way. Zeke had dreamed for too long. After tearing his mouth away, Zeke kissed and nipped every place he could reach as he pounded Korey's ass.

Korey reached between them and tugged at his cock. Zeke had to watch. Sitting back on his heels, he held Korey's thighs, pumping inside the man as he watched him jack off. Between the heat squeezing his dick and the erotic picture Korey painted, the pressure beating at Zeke's crown was winning. He needed relief. Korey moaned and writhed beneath him without shame.

"You're so goddamn sexy." With the first growled words between them, Zeke couldn't stop. "I need to see you come again. You're so perfect on my dick, I won't make it much longer. I knew you would be this way."

Korey's motions quickened. Zeke couldn't tear his gaze away from the way Korey's crown disappeared inside his fist over and over again. Pressure drew his balls up tight, crawling up his shaft, and beat at his crown. Zeke couldn't slow. He reached for the ecstasy that Korey's tight ass promised. Korey's muscles tensed. His ass clamped down on Zeke's dick with enough force he almost crippled Zeke. Korey's body jerked as his orgasm hit. His ass spasmed, milking Zeke into oblivion. Lights popped behind Zeke's eyes as he came, making him wonder if he was having a stroke. He couldn't breathe. Wave after wave of pleasure consumed him. In that moment, Korey owned him in a way no one else ever had. That had been true before he'd been inside Korey, but now, Zeke couldn't see a future without him.

He covered Korey's mouth with his as he filled the condom covering his dick. Korey's tongue battling with his was the only thing stopping all Zeke's confessions. Tomorrow, he'd face the consequences of what he'd done. Right now, he needed Korey.

TWO

KOREY KNEW HE WAS ALONE BEFORE HE OPENED his eyes. It wasn't the yawning sensation of Zeke's powerful presence missing from the bed as much as it was the smell of coffee wafting through the house. A smile pulled at the corners of Korey's mouth. Zeke didn't drink coffee. That meant he'd made it for him. Korey stretched, reveling in the ache in his muscles. He didn't want to think. If he did, he'd wonder where they were headed from here or if last night had been a fluke. Would Zeke kiss him good morning or pretend nothing happened? Korey wasn't sure he could go back to acting as if Zeke wasn't the love of his life. What other choice did he have if Zeke didn't acknowledge what they'd done? None whatsoever. Zeke took care of him in every way. It wasn't like Korey could get angry and walk away. Zeke held all the cards. So much for not thinking.

Giving up, Korey rolled from the bed and headed for his room. The steam from his blazing hot shower cleared his head. He would follow Zeke's lead and hope for the best. That didn't mean he wouldn't try to look as sexy as possible in the meantime. Korey chose his outfit with care and made sure his hair was perfect. He'd wanted Zeke for long enough he'd mentally noted each time the man's gaze had lingered longer than usual. It happened more often in a certain pair of jeans. Korey pulled them on. He might not have the right words or a leg to stand on, but Korey would fight with what God gave him.

With a deep breath for courage, Korey headed for the kitchen. It was empty. Korey's hands shook as he poured himself some coffee. Fuck. He didn't want to search the house like a desperate stalker. Instead, he leaned against the counter and sipped the warm liquid while doing his damnedest to think of nothing. He didn't taste a thing. Korey was too nervous.

Zeke finally cleared the door, wearing a faded red t-shirt that hugged his muscles and worn jeans that cupped his every asset. Korey almost choked on his drink. He swallowed hard to keep from falling into a coughing fit. Zeke didn't look his way.

"I thought I'd drive you to school."

Korey gripped his cup between his hands and willed Zeke to look at him. "Okay."

Zeke glanced at the clock. "You might want to hurry. It's almost time for your Psych class."

Korey thought he'd prepared for this. Zeke's refusal to look at him hurt more than expected. "All right." Korey set his cup aside and grabbed his stuff while keeping his gaze carefully averted from Zeke. The pains in his chest might be a heart attack, but probably not. He worried if he kept staring at Zeke while Zeke made a show of not looking his way, Korey might die.

Zeke led the way to his black Jeep Wrangler Unlimited.

Korey watched the man's ass.

Zeke tossed a glance over his shoulder but didn't meet Korey's gaze. "If you find out your test results today, text me and let me know."

"Okay." Fuck. It was like Korey only knew two responses. He'd sworn he'd deal if Zeke pretended nothing happened. Now that the time was here, Korey could barely breathe past the pain. The ride to school only took fifteen minutes. It felt like hours in the uncomfortable silence. Korey never once glanced Zeke's way. His gaze stayed glued on the road, seeing nothing. All his concentration went to breathing. By the time Zeke pulled into the parking lot, Korey was ready to leap from the car. His hand was on the handle before the Jeep rolled to a stop.

"Wait," Zeke said, snagging Korey's arm before he could slip from the vehicle. Hope exploded through Korey's chest at the first contact of skin on skin. It died a swift death at Zeke's pained expression. "Look, last night was a mistake."

Ouch. "I see." That was a lie. Korey saw nothing.

"When you moved out here to go to Stanford, your mom had just passed. Then, Charlie died. You moved in with me, and I just think you haven't had time to get out there. Do things. I've done everything. So, last night won't happen again. Okay?"

There were no words. Equally, all oxygen seemed scarce. He already knew everything Zeke said without the recap of how much he'd lost. Korey didn't need the reminder he was alone in the world. Most of all, he didn't need the revelation that Zeke didn't belong to him in any way either. Korey feared if he opened his mouth, all his pain would pour out and drown them. Instead, he gave Zeke a sharp nod and walked away. It seemed he needed to make new plans for his life. Plans that didn't include Zeke.

KOREY DIDN'T SHOW after school. The more minutes that passed without Korey appearing in his usual chair, the more violent Zeke's strikes against the punch pads Maverick held became.

Maverick shook out his hands. "Damn, Zeke. What's gotten into you today?"

"Nothing. I have a match in two days. Put your hands up."

Maverick tucked the punch pads beneath his arm and shook his head. "If you're bent on hurting yourself before making it to the cage, you can get someone else to help with that."

Zeke fought the urge to put his fist through the wall. The image of Korey's devastation after Zeke's speech this morning wouldn't leave Zeke's head. Now the man hadn't shown for his ride home and Maverick was pissed at him. All he ever did was fuck things up.

Giving up, he headed for his locker and dug out his phone. Maybe something happened and Korey had called. There were no messages or missed calls. Zeke texted him. He didn't want to leave and miss him.

Zeke: *Where are you?*

Thankfully, Korey responded right away.

Korey: *Home. I had some stuff to do, so I caught the bus.*

Zeke: *Okay. I didn't want to leave here and you show up needing a ride.*

Korey: *Nope. I'm good.*

Zeke: *I'll see you in a few. What would you like for dinner? I'll pick something up.*

Korey: *I won't be here for dinner, but thanks.*

He wouldn't be there? Korey was always there. Zeke shoved his phone in his bag and headed for the door. He needed to get home. Something was going on, and Zeke didn't doubt for a second it had everything to do with last night. His goddamn dick always got him in trouble. He should never have touched Korey. Zeke rubbed the spot in his chest that ached at the thought of losing Korey from his life. Last night had been the greatest night of his life. He wanted to rush home and kiss Korey again and beg the man to give him everything. That wasn't fair. Korey should hear it all and then decide if he still wanted Zeke. Zeke shouldn't have touched Korey without all his cards on the table.

He drove home faster than necessary. Thankfully, he didn't run across any police. His car barely stopped rolling before he was out and headed inside the house. At the first sight of Korey packing, Zeke knew he'd been right to rush home.

"Where are you going?"

Korey startled, clutching his heart. "Holy crap. Make some noise next time. You almost gave me a heart attack."

He still wore the jeans Zeke loved. They were slightly worn and cupped Korey's ass. As always, Zeke forgot all the reasons they shouldn't be together while staring at Korey. "You didn't answer me. Where are you going?"

Korey's gaze skirted away. "Out."

"You need an overnight bag to go out?"

Korey's chest expanded. His gaze found Zeke's. "I accepted Maverick's invitation to go to Vegas. We're leaving later tonight."

Zeke blinked while trying to control his temper. He cleared his throat before responding. "You didn't want to go with me?"

A muscle jumped in Korey's jaw. "I don't want to be someone's mistake. So far, Maverick has been straightforward about what he wants. I'd prefer to go with someone who won't regret me."

"Maverick will break your heart," Zeke said with more spite than he intended. Zeke could never regret Korey. He equally couldn't believe the man would leave his bed and head straight for another.

"He won't be the first," Korey shot back. His mark hit home.

Zeke couldn't stop. "Maverick only wants one thing."

Korey shrugged. "At least he wants me and doesn't see me as a naïve child. He doesn't look at me and see an obligation to my brother."

"It sounds like maybe you should go live with Maverick and he can support you while you finish medical school." As the words left his lips, Zeke regretted them, but he didn't stop. He didn't know how one person could be so goddamn blind. Did Korey honestly think Zeke had kept him around all this time for Charlie's sake? He could've set Korey up in an apartment and checked on him every few months.

Instead of flying into a rage, as Zeke would've done in Korey's place, Korey dug through his stuff and came out with his checkbook. He scratched something on the paper before tearing off a check and handing it over. Zeke reached for it without thought. He glanced at the check. It was for fifty thousand. His brows snapped together. "What's this?"

"It's what's left of Charlie's life insurance money. I'll have my stuff out by the end of next week."

"This money is supposed to keep you in books and whatever else extra stuff you need for school until you graduate."

Korey shrugged as he snatched up his overnight bag. "Now it'll go to cover having me under your roof the past two years. I'm sorry I stayed where I wasn't welcome. If I'd been in my right mind when Charlie died, I might've realized it sooner."

Zeke's temper shot through the roof, making his earlier outburst seem minuscule by comparison. "You know good goddamn well you have always been welcome here. Take this." He tried handing the check back. Korey sidestepped him.

"I don't know anything anymore."

Zeke ripped the check to shreds and tossed it at Korey's chest. "You're the smartest goddamn idiot I've ever met."

Korey finally snapped. He tossed his bag aside. "No shit, Zeke. You think I don't know that? I'm the one who sat around here for two years, waiting for you to notice I fucking love you, while you were wishing I'd figure out I'm a goddamn burden. Tell me what you want because I can't pretend anymore. I want to be with someone who wants me too. I don't want to be someone's mistake."

Zeke's brain didn't move past Korey's claim of loving him. His mouth opened. No sound emerged. He snapped his teeth together.

Korey snorted. It was an ugly sound. "That's what I thought," Korey said, scooping up his bag, obviously intent on leaving. Maybe Zeke didn't have Korey's courage with words, but that didn't mean he didn't feel. Unfortunately, by the time his brain found an argument, Korey was gone. Zeke raced through the house. He made it to the garage in enough time to see Korey pull away. The most ridiculous thought hit in his time of desperation. He should've bought Korey a new car while he'd had a chance. Korey had a brake light out.

UGLY RAGE MIXED with crippling pain to wreck Korey's mind. He drove with no real destination in mind. Vegas was no longer an option. Maverick was

Zeke's friend. The only way Korey would ever get past this was to cut all ties. He couldn't leave Maverick hanging, though. That wouldn't be fair. He equally couldn't back out of something as huge as a trip to Vegas via text. That wasn't cool.

With a sigh, he changed lanes and headed for the address Maverick had given him. Korey tried like hell to keep his mind blank. He was half a breath away from falling apart. Since Charlie's death, Zeke had been Korey's rock. Now there was nothing standing between him and the massive loss. Despair was a tidal wave waiting to drown him. Each breath came harder than the last. Korey tried counting backwards from a hundred while measuring his breaths. A set of townhomes came into view, making Korey realize he'd somehow made it to Maverick's without dying. He found building R and pulled into a parking spot next to a familiar-looking red Dodge Ram. For a moment, he stared at nothing and absorbed the silence of the night. The last thing he needed was to fall apart the second Maverick opened the door. Korey squeezed his eyes shut, hoping to clear the haze coating them. It didn't help. Everything hurt.

Fuck it. He needed this chore done so he could find a quiet place to fall apart—no witnesses. He eyed the yellow siding of the two-story buildings. It seemed like a quiet place. He wondered if they had anything available for rent. Korey snorted. He probably couldn't afford it. Even if Zeke never accepted Charlie's life insurance money, fifty thousand would only last him so long without a job. He still had years left of school. Between interning, studying, and a million other things he had coming his way, there was no way he could pay his bills by himself. All that bullshit paled in comparison to the destruction Zeke had wreaked on his heart. He was in tatters. Concentrating on his monetary problems was the only thing keeping him sane. Korey stopped outside Maverick's door. After bending at the waist, Korey braced his hands on his knees and sucked air. Hyperventilating was right around the corner. He could feel it. Everything looked insurmountable and piled on top of losing Zeke. Korey couldn't deal. Everything hurt. He straightened, determined to get through this life. As his knuckles skimmed the door, Korey tried swallowing down his pain. He half expected to choke on it.

The door swung open. Maverick was shirtless. Korey almost forgot why he was there. Damn. Maverick was beautiful. Maverick eyed Korey while wearing a self-satisfied smile. He motioned Korey inside. "Come in."

Korey waved off the suggestion. "No. I can't stay. Sorry. I hate doing this on such short notice, but I just stopped by to tell you I can't go to Vegas with you this weekend." Korey couldn't meet Maverick's stare.

"That's okay. Are you all right? Would you like to come in?"

Korey imagined he looked every bit as broken as he felt. He couldn't even work up a lie. "No. I have to find a new place to live before it gets too late."

"Damn. That doesn't sound good. Come in. You can stay with me until you're settled."

Despite the shit night he'd had, Korey managed a smile. He finally met Maverick's stare. "I couldn't, but thanks."

Maverick snagged his arm and dragged him inside. "I wasn't asking. No offense, but you look like hell. Zeke would kill me if I let you drive away this upset."

Korey tried going back out the door at the mention of Zeke's name. "Fuck Zeke. He doesn't care about me, and I don't need anyone telling him where I am."

"Nope," Maverick said, blocking his exit. Korey

might've tried pushing his way out, but then he would've had to touch Maverick's sexy bare chest and that couldn't happen. "You're staying," Maverick said, sounding firm. "I didn't say a word about telling Zeke where you are. You're a grown man. He doesn't need to know where you are at all times."

Maverick's words had the tension draining from Korey's shoulders. He nodded. "Thanks. It's been a rough day. If you're cool with me crashing on your couch, I'd be forever grateful and out of your hair in the morning."

Maverick motioned toward the couch. "I have a guest bedroom and you're not in my hair. Things haven't exactly been great for me either today. You're doing me a favor by agreeing to keep me company."

Even though Korey felt certain Maverick was only placating him, he was too upset to care. He moved to the couch and sat. "Why was your day bad?" Korey needed to concentrate on something other than his issues.

Maverick chose the opposite end of the couch and kicked his feet up onto the coffee table. For a moment, he stared into space, looking thoughtful. Korey's breath stuttered as he caught a glimpse behind Maverick's usual cocky mask. He was broken. Just like Korey.

Maverick shook his head. "It's nothing." He flashed Korey a smile. "Tell me about Zeke. I know he didn't put you out, so why are you looking for a place to live?"

Korey dropped his head back on the couch and eyed the ceiling. Without thought, he crossed his arms over his chest to protect his heart. No matter how hard he searched his mind, Korey couldn't think of a place to start that didn't make him sound like a damn fool. "I put myself out," he said finally. "Zeke never would've done it and it needed to be done."

"How long have you been in love with him?"

Korey blinked back tears at the question. Damn, it hurt. A snort escaped him. There was no sense in lying. Everything was lost. "Since day one. God," Korey breathed. "I'm such a dumbass."

"No. He is."

Maverick's claim had Korey meeting the man's gaze. He needed someone to tell him he wasn't being childish or stupid.

Maverick didn't let him down. "A man like Zeke doesn't keep someone around and give them as much as he's given you unless he wants something in return. The way he watches you, I'd say he wants everything from you."

Korey snorted and went back to staring at the

ceiling. "He's already had all of me. Now he's over it." There was no sense in playing the innocent at this point. "Fuck." He needed to move on. He met Maverick's gaze. "If you already knew about Zeke and me, why did you ask me to go to Vegas with you?"

Maverick eyed him, going as far as to tilt his head to one side, looking for something only he understood. "I think we're a lot alike, and maybe we'd be better together."

"Better than what?"

A sad smile touched Maverick's lips. "Better than with someone who's never been told no. Someone whose money has bought them whatever and whoever they want. Just better," Maverick said, sounding sad. He looked away and crossed his arms over his chest, mimicking Korey's heart-shielding pose. "Yesterday... I don't know. I saw something in you." He shook his head and flashed Korey a sad smile. "Never mind. You're hot. We're young. Why don't we go ahead and hit Vegas? You can leave before Zeke's fight, and get your things out while he's otherwise occupied. I'd make it worth your while."

Despite everything, a smile tugged at Korey's lips. "I'm tempted to take you up on that just so I'll stop feeling like I've been kicked in the balls."

"Let's do it then," Maverick said, shifting to his feet.

"But," Korey said, stopping him. "That wouldn't be fair to you."

Maverick's usual cocky demeanor returned. "Babe, I'm eyes wide open and willing." His smile slipped. "You'd be helping me too."

A loud sigh escaped Korey. He had a bad feeling he would regret this one day. "All right. Let's go," Korey said, coming to his feet. It wasn't like he had anything left to lose. Zeke had already stolen everything from Korey a long time ago.

THREE

ZEKE: HERE'S MY HOTEL INFORMATION IN CASE *you need me.*

ZEKE: *What time does your flight leave and where are you staying?*

ZEKE: *I'm not trying to pry. Have a safe flight.*

ZEKE: *EVEN A "GO FUCK YOURSELF" is better than not answering.*

ZEKE: *Okay. Guess I'll go fuck myself then.*

THERE WAS no such thing as a quiet spot inside an arena with twenty thousand screaming fans in attendance. Zeke's fight wasn't the only one taking place. He stayed hidden inside the back room he'd been assigned. Security had been posted outside his door. Zeke couldn't stop pacing. It was impossible to not be nervous before a bout. An official had already signed off on his tape. Zeke would have to repeat the process outside the cage, but for now, he had nothing to do but wait. Was Korey out there? Since the man had been ignoring Zeke's texts, there was no way for him to know. He could text Maverick, but that smacked too much of desperation. If he looked at things too closely, Zeke already felt like an idiot for falling for a man fourteen years younger than him. He'd never thought he'd be that guy, taking care of a younger man and still trying to fake at not being in love. What the fuck was wrong with him? Korey had admitted to loving him, and Zeke had let him walk away. He couldn't stop trying to kick his own ass over that one. Now he was moments away from a huge match, and Korey wasn't with him. Zeke had no one to blame but himself.

"It's time," Hendrix, Zeke's corner man, said, pulling him from his thoughts.

Zeke locked his jaw and gave Hendrix a sharp nod. He cleared the door to ear-blasting screams. Then, all sound died away, muffled by his tunnel vision. Zeke was in fight mode. This was his job. He'd been training for months. This was his fourth title match, and he'd held on to the title after each one before now. Zeke wouldn't let this next guy take his strap. He paused outside the cage for inspection. The second judge signed off on his tape before Zeke made his way inside. Nothing except the sound of each breath he took penetrated his focus.

Deshawn Oliver had a longer reach. It wouldn't mean shit. The man was also ten years younger than Zeke. That didn't matter at all. Zeke was better. Rules were read. Zeke tuned it all out. He knew them by heart. The match began, and Zeke fell into wait and see mode. Sometimes, striking hard and fast wasn't the best move. Tonight was one of those nights. He planned to let Deshawn tire himself out. Zeke had the stamina. Then, Deshawn dipped his left shoulder, teasing Zeke with an opening. He took it, striking out and connecting with Deshawn's jaw. The man made him pay by landing a blow to Zeke's right cheek. He felt the skin split, but no pain penetrated the adrenaline pumping through his veins. Zeke pulled off a leg sweep before Deshawn regained his balance. The man went down but popped back up.

Five rounds went by with more of the same. They each got their hits in. Zeke already knew he was winning in scores. Deshawn would make his move soon. He couldn't win with hits at this point. The man needed to take Zeke out. That made him twice as dangerous. Zeke's muscles felt the wear of battle, but he had enough strength to last. Deshawn had a tell. He led with his right foot. Zeke saw his next move coming a half second before the man tried taking him to the mat. Zeke dodged, unbalancing him, and struck before the man could recover. With a shove and a twist, Zeke had Deshawn pinned. He kept the man's arm rotated at an odd angle, putting all his strength behind the move. He didn't see Deshawn tap, but the bell rang. He'd won by submission. The roar of the crowd rushed back to his ears, nearly deafening him. His arms were raised, and a microphone shoved beneath his nose. In truth, Zeke had no clue what he said. His gaze moved from one seat to the next, searching. He knew it was unlikely he'd spot Korey in the crowd. His brain refused to give up the hunt. Nothing mattered if he couldn't share it with Korey.

Everything passed in a blur as he was shuffled from interview to interview. Still, it seemed like time moved at half its pace. All Zeke wanted was to find Korey. He had no clue where the man was. Giving in, he texted Maverick.

Zeke: *Where are you?*

Maverick: *Sudden Skies bar inside The Luna hotel.*

Zeke: *I might catch up with you there.*

Maverick: *I'll be here. BTW, Congrats. You were awesome.*

The Luna hotel was within walking distance. Zeke pulled up the hood on his hoodie, put his head down, and made his way through the crowd. No one tried stopping him. Of course, he imagined he didn't give off a friendly vibe. Zeke's man was here with someone else. That was something he couldn't accept. No matter how tired he was, he had to get to Korey.

He liked Maverick, but Zeke had no qualms about stealing Korey out from underneath him. Maverick hadn't spent the last two years loving Korey. Zeke had.

When he cleared the door, Zeke spotted Maverick right away. Korey was nowhere in sight. He cut through the crowd. Zeke didn't waste time with pleasantries. "Where's Korey?"

Maverick turned. His bright smile fell when his gaze landed on Zeke, making Zeke wonder if he looked as deadly as he felt. "He cancelled on me, saying he had to move this weekend."

Zeke's throat swelled. "What?"

Maverick nodded, as if Zeke had asked a yes or no question. "Surprised me too. I thought you would've said something if Korey was moving out."

"He said something about it, but I thought he'd change his mind," Zeke said absently. He was over five hundred miles away. It would take time to get home even if he raced there this second.

Maverick's gaze moved over Zeke's face, as if searching for answers. "Let me buy you a drink."

Zeke shook his head.

The line between Maverick's brows deepened. "You won. You should be celebrating. Hell, it wasn't even me and I'm celebrating."

"No, thanks." He couldn't stop shifting from foot to foot. Korey wasn't there. Zeke needed to fix things. Nothing else mattered.

"Am I trespassing?" Maverick asked, catching Zeke off guard. "I mean, I've always assumed you thought of Korey as a little brother, but I don't know. Since I invited him here, you've been acting weird. I thought we were friends."

Zeke didn't know how to respond. He couldn't deny he'd treated Maverick differently. Zeke searched his mind for something that wasn't a lie. "Of course we're friends. Thanks for showing up, and I have no claim on Korey. We just had a fight."

The way Maverick nodded and worried at his lips screamed he didn't think Zeke was being honest. Maverick didn't back down. "Just so you know, I'm not toying with him. I wouldn't do that, knowing how close the two of you are. He's a great guy. I genuinely like him. In truth, we don't meet a lot of nice guys, doing what we do."

Maverick said all the right things. If it was anyone other than Korey, Zeke would be thrilled for the guy. He couldn't do this. "I have to go." Zeke headed for the door without any further explanation. He knew he looked crazy. Zeke wasn't sure someone shouldn't be calling his mental stability into question.

He made it ten feet before Maverick caught up with him. "Zeke. Hold up."

Zeke turned, barely stamping down his impatience.

"Come on," Maverick said, slapping Zeke on the back and maneuvering him toward the door. "My sister works for Western Air. She can pull some strings and have you home before the end of the night. Maybe you can catch Korey before he gets all his stuff moved out. Then your dumb ass can tell him you love him before things are fucked up beyond all repair."

Zeke never considered denying it. "Am I that obvious?"

"It's a little sickening. Plus, you just told an arena filled with twenty-thousand people that Korey was the reason for everything you do," Maverick said with a laugh. "I thought you'd surely break, with me all on your toes, but nope. For fuck's sake, man. You're one of the toughest bastards I know. Sack up and tell the man how you feel." He paused and glanced over, meeting Zeke's stare. His tone turned serious. "Or I will steal him. For real, he deserves better than getting strung along for the rest of his life."

Later, Zeke might look back and have some strong feelings of hate over this conversation. For now, all he needed was to get to Korey before he lost the man for good. Maverick had the connections to make that happen. Everything else could wait.

———

THERE WAS ONLY one night left in the house he shared with Zeke. The place felt empty without Zeke's powerful presence. Still, Korey couldn't convince himself to leave a second before necessary. Korey curled up in their chair. He was pissed. Fury ate at his gut and clawed at his brain. Korey wanted to scratch off his skin. Most of all, he wished Zeke hurt even a quarter as much as he did.

At any point over the past two years, Zeke could've spoken up and told Korey to leave. He sure as shit could've done it before fucking Korey. Before wrecking Korey. Oddly, leaving Maverick behind in Vegas hadn't been easy. Maverick was hot and fun. He was the perfect person to help Korey move on, but Korey couldn't stand on the sidelines in Vegas and cheer for Zeke. He needed to get his shit the fuck out while Zeke was otherwise engaged. Was Zeke occupied elsewhere? Would he find someone to share his bed tonight? Korey imagined Zeke always found one or two people to fuck when Korey wasn't around. Bastard. There was nothing Korey could do to magically transform into the person Zeke wanted him to be. He couldn't be older, worldlier, or less fucked up. There was no chance for them. Korey hurt. Everything pained him. If he had any sense, he'd stand up now and walk away from the hell he wallowed in. Tomorrow was soon enough. When the sun came up, he'd do better.

With that plan firmly in place, Korey headed for his bedroom. He had a few things left to pack. As he crossed the threshold into the space Zeke had given him, the air seemed to thin. He fought for oxygen. Korey sat on the bed and tried calming his racing heart. His gaze landed on the framed photos beside his bed. One stood out. Zeke and Charlie wore camo and smiled for the camera. They looked happy. Korey's stomach cramped. He should leave the picture for Zeke. If Charlie hadn't been straight, Korey might hate the way he'd obviously made Zeke happy. Korey always seemed to make Zeke scowl more than he made him smile.

He picked up the frame and headed for Zeke's room. As he set the picture on the table beneath Zeke's bedroom window, he couldn't release the frame. Going down on his haunches, Korey leaned his chin on his forearm and stared closer at the image. His brother's gleaming smile stared back at him. Korey always tried hard not to think about the brother he lost. As he stared at him now, Korey's throat swelled. The past two-and-a-half years of his life had been hell. He'd lost everyone who mattered. Now Zeke would be gone too. He couldn't help but blame Charlie for putting him in this position.

"I hate you for leaving me with another fucking mess," Korey whispered. A tear slipped down his cheek. He loved his brother. The man hadn't been perfect. He was never around. When their mom had her first stroke six years ago, Charlie had left her to Korey's care. Somehow, Korey had pulled off taking care of everything while still managing to get an academic scholarship to Stanford. Then, their mom had passed, and Charlie had—once again—left Korey to handle everything. His brother had promised things would be better for Korey in California. He'd lied.

After pushing to his feet, Korey took a step back and sat on Zeke's bed. Another tear followed the first. He was so fucking tired. Korey closed his eyes and curled onto his side. He swiped at his cheeks and sniffed. Life was exhausting. Zeke had been a tiny hint of light in an otherwise dark existence. Now he was gone too.

KOREY'S CAR wasn't in the garage. Still, Zeke burst through the door, praying he was there. The silence he met was beyond deafening. The house felt emptier than he could've imagined. Every breath he took seemed to reverberate off the walls and assault his ears. Even knowing the truth didn't stop him from checking Korey's room. The furniture was there, but it had been stripped bare of all personal items. The drawers and closet were empty. There was nothing left of Korey's usual mess of products in the bathroom.

As Zeke's feet crossed the threshold of his bedroom, his steps slowed. A familiar picture of Charlie and him sat on the table beneath the window. Zeke recognized it as the one that had been on the table by Korey's bed. A sheet of spiral notebook paper haphazardly torn was tucked beneath the edge of the frame. Zeke's hand shook as he retrieved it. His eyes burned as he read.

Zeke,

Thank you for giving me two years of peace when I needed them the most. I'm sure your tolerance of my bullshit more than surpassed Charlie's expectations. I'm sorry our friendship ended on such a horrible note. More than that, I'm sorry I thought we were friends while you felt you were being used. I left another check on the fridge. Please cash it. I never meant to take advantage of you. Maybe one day you'll look back on me in a better light, but I don't think that'll happen if you don't cash that check. I'm prouder to have known you than you'll ever understand. There are too many words in my head to know how to end this, so I'll just say, stay well.

—Korey

Fuck Korey for thinking he could walk away with a note. They weren't done until Zeke said they were and that was never. After balling up the paper and tossing it on the floor, Zeke dug out his phone and headed to the kitchen to tear up another check. He would find Korey. When he did, he'd turn the boy over his knee for ever thinking any of the bullshit in that note was true.

MAVERICK HAD PASSED SHITFACED two hours ago and moved into a territory of drunkenness he'd never known before. He prayed he hadn't made a mistake by helping Zeke get to Korey in a hurry. They loved each other. Someone deserved happiness, but he shouldn't have gotten involved.

A familiar tingle ran up his spine. Maverick fought the urge to turn his head. Zander was here. Somewhere. Watching him. Before he could catch the bartender's eye to get another drink, Maverick found himself sandwiched between two gigantic men. His heart fell. He'd known this was coming.

"Mr. Kapra requests the pleasure of your company," the man to his left said. There was no hiding his heavy Russian accent.

A snort escaped Maverick before he could call it back. "Tell Zander he can go fuck himself."

Something warm pressed against his back. Maverick's eyes fell closed as the familiar scent of expensive cologne overcame him. "Why would I do that when I can fuck you?" The softly spoken question brushed the shell of Maverick's ear. The two behemoths disappeared, leaving Maverick alone with the man who always crushed him. He should've jumped a flight with Zeke while he had the chance. Now it was too late. Maybe it always had been. His phone buzzed, saving him from acknowledging Zander. It took a moment for his eyes to focus so he could read Zeke's text.

Zeke: *He's gone. I need your help.*

Maverick: *Give me a minute.*

In truth, he needed like five minutes to drunkenly scroll through his messages until he found Korey's number.

Maverick: *Did you get settled?*

Korey: *Yeah. I'm at Hotel 10 on Monroe in room 114. They'll let me pay by the week until I find an apartment. Thanks for everything.*

Maverick: *No worries. Keep me posted.*

Korey: *Okay.*

After blinking several times at his phone, Maverick managed to copy and paste Korey's message in a message to Zeke. With that out of the way, there was nothing left for him to do than focus on the ice-blue eyes that haunted him every second of the day.

"Did you say something about fucking me?" If so, now was the time. Maverick was too plastered to feel.

That was the only way he could handle Zander touching him.

"That depends," Zander said, sounding harder than usual. "Did you bring that child with you to Vegas to taunt me?"

A thousand responses raced to Maverick's lips, even he wasn't sure which one would fall. All Maverick knew was there wasn't enough alcohol in all of Vegas to drown the way he felt when Zander came around. Nothing or no one scared him more.

KOREY HADN'T MADE it through the night at Zeke's. It was too hard. The man's presence was everywhere, suffocating Korey with love he'd never have. Everywhere he'd looked, Zeke had been there. The hotel was noisy as fuck, but Korey reveled in every loud car, yell, pounding music, and slamming car door. He'd never felt more alone in the world. On his side, facing the wall, Korey stared at nothing. He wanted to feel nothing. He hadn't cried when Charlie died. Now that Zeke was gone, Korey felt like the tears wouldn't stop coming, as if Zeke had been the glue holding him together. He hurt everywhere.

Korey closed his eyes and held his breath, hoping to calm the inner storm raging inside him. Warmth engulfed him. Zeke's familiar scent surrounded him. "I'm sorry," Zeke said against his ear. He touched his lips to the spot beneath Korey's ear. "Please don't leave me."

Korey's throat burned. Zeke was there. He'd been so close to embracing the fact that he'd never see the man again. Korey wanted to be surprised the man had—somehow—silently broken into his hotel room, but nothing about Zeke shocked Korey. The man always got his way. It seemed there should be a million things for Korey to say. His voice wouldn't work.

Zeke urged Korey onto his back. Korey fought the temptation to squeeze his eyes shut against the sight of him. There was a cut under Zeke's right eye. Korey's fingers automatically brushed beneath it.

"I know it's your job, but I don't like when you get hurt."

Intense emotions swam in Zeke's gaze, making Korey's heart race. Zeke wiped away the moisture from beneath Korey's eyes. "You're hurting me right now. Leaving wasn't part of our deal," Zeke said, his voice turning harder by the second. "You were supposed to stay. I was supposed to retire and spend my days bragging about my sexy husband the doctor."

Each breath came harder than the last. Korey wondered if his mind had snapped. Zeke spoke like he'd always meant for them to be together. "You said I was a mistake."

"No," Zeke said with a shake of his head. "I said the other night was a mistake. You're the best thing that's ever happened to me. But I shouldn't have touched you without telling you everything about me first. You deserve to be seduced and spoiled by someone you know everything about. I don't want to steal your options. I want you to choose me even after you've seen all my cards and know all my bullshit."

"I know you." He did. Maybe he hadn't heard every story Zeke had to tell, but he knew him.

Zeke shook his head. A sad smile touched his lips. "You don't." He brushed Korey's hair away from his face. "Do you know how I met your brother?"

Korey had never thought to ask. He didn't like thinking about Charlie. "No."

"He was my sobriety coach. I paid him so I

wouldn't have to go to a treatment facility after I was found passed out in my car by the police."

"He was your best friend," Korey argued, not wanting to hear Zeke's life had been anything other than perfect.

"He was," Zeke agreed, "but not at first. In the beginning, I was his job. I tore out my knee fighting and got addicted to pain killers. Becoming an addict happened before I realized it." Zeke's mouth lifted in one corner. "You have an amazing career ahead of you. I'm so damn proud of you, and I don't ever want to become an embarrassment to you."

Korey didn't want to make light of Zeke's confession, but the man hadn't said anything he couldn't deal with yet. "Is that all?"

A small smile touched Zeke's lips. "I'm fourteen years older than you."

Korey bit the inside of his cheek to keep from laughing. "That, I've known."

Zeke's expression turned serious. "I'm in love with you."

That, he hadn't known. Korey blinked. The hot press of tears behind his eyes threatened to overcome him again. He had to clear his throat to speak. "I'm in love with you too."

"I want you to come home."

Korey rolled from the bed. "I want you to show me the rest of your injuries. You didn't go five rounds and end up with only one cut." He flipped the bathroom light on, determined to see all of Zeke.

Zeke moved fast for someone who'd already been in one fight tonight. His chest collided with Korey's back. The man's arms encircled Korey's waist. "You have some questions to answer first."

Happiness made Korey bold. "Strip and I'll answer while you do."

Zeke released him. Korey leaned against the bathroom counter, enjoying the show. He pulled his shirt up and over his head, revealing bruised ribs. "How did you know my match lasted five rounds?"

"Maverick texted me the details."

Zeke tossed his shirt aside and crowded Korey against the vanity. "No more texting with Maverick."

"We're friends," Korey argued. "He talked me out of heading back to Alabama. Otherwise, I might have walked away from everything here and disappeared for good. He knows it's you I love."

"Tell me you'll come home," Zeke ordered, letting his earlier demand go. His fingers brushed Korey's jaw. The man made it damn hard to hold a conversation. He made a lot of things hard.

"Tell me you love me again," Korey whispered, needing more.

Zeke didn't hesitate giving in. "I love you. Come home."

"Only if you kiss me." Because Korey thought he'd die if didn't taste Zeke soon.

"Now's the time for you to ask for anything, and all you want is a kiss?"

Korey amended his request. "You should also take off your pants."

"Done," Zeke said before touching his lips to the corner of Korey's mouth.

"If you ever tell me I'm a mistake again, I'm punching you in the dick," Korey warned. He turned his head, capturing Zeke's lips before the man changed his mind. The man's kiss was everything it had been the other night and more, because this time, he knew he had Zeke's heart. Zeke's kiss was overpowering. Korey submitted to the man's assault. Zeke softened. Over the past two years, Korey might not have been Zeke's lover. That didn't mean Korey didn't know him. He understood how to get his way with Zeke. The more he ceded to Zeke, the more Zeke melted, becoming sweeter by the second. "Pants," Korey reminded him between kisses.

Zeke's hands went to the button on his jeans.

Korey could've done it, but he wanted to watch Zeke strip. However, there was no stopping his fingers from finding the man's abs before moving to the pads of Zeke's chest. Zeke was hard all over. He was like velvet over steel. All the times Korey had stared at Zeke and fantasized about touching him rose to the surface. Zeke's breath shuddered around Korey's tongue as Korey skimmed his hands down Zeke's sides.

"Perfect," Zeke breathed, skimming his lips from Korey's mouth to his jaw. "So fucking gorgeous," Zeke added, continuing to rain praise on Korey. "No one will believe you're with me for anything other than my money."

A chuckle rose in Korey's throat. There wasn't a person alive who wouldn't lust for Zeke's body after a single glance. "My sugar fighter."

Zeke nipped at Korey's lips but never let Korey catch him for a deeper kiss. "Always."

As Zeke pushed his jeans down his hips, Korey bent at the waist, chasing after him and refusing to give up the man's mouth. A soft laugh escaped Zeke. The sound vibrated against Korey's lips. His breath caught. "I love you." Zeke had given him the freedom to say the words, and now Korey never wanted to stop confessing his feelings. They'd been pent up too long.

Zeke kicked out of his clothes and came at Korey with more aggression than Korey expected. He gasped at the assault. Zeke tore at Korey's clothes, and his teeth sank into Korey's bottom lip. They fought to get closer—skin on skin with no barriers. When their bare chests met and then their erections bumped, they calmed. This was where they were meant to be. Zeke gently spun Korey in his arms, forcing Korey's gaze toward the mirror. "Look at us together."

A sickness grew inside Korey at the reflection of Zeke holding him. His stomach cramped with need. There would never be such thing as too much of Zeke.

"We're perfect together," Zeke said, stroking Korey's stomach and heading south.

Korey swallowed. His throat was like sandpaper. Korey held on to the counter like it was the glue holding his sanity together. Korey couldn't look away from Zeke. His eyes couldn't give up the sight of the sexy arms surrounding him. Everything about Zeke was cut to perfection. The man was beautiful. Their gazes met in the mirror. Pre-cum rolled down his length.

Zeke palmed Korey's cock. "Do you jack off to fantasies of me as often as I stroke myself to thoughts of you?"

"If you mean almost daily, then yes," Korey answered honestly. Korey's chest expanded. Zeke lightly stroked him, torturing him with the promise of more.

"What do I do to you in these fantasies?"

"Everything," Korey gasped as Zeke tightened his hold on Korey's cock.

"Do I make you suffer, dragging out your pleasure?"

Korey was too horny to be embarrassed. "Yes."

"Am I ever on my knees?" Zeke asked against Korey's shoulder. His lips brushed Korey's skin with every syllable.

"No."

Zeke paused, as if shocked by Korey's response. "Do you think I won't drop right here and take you down my throat?"

Without an ounce of shame, Korey held Zeke's gaze in the mirror. "That's not how I picture you when I imagine you sucking my dick. You're always on your back, and I'm always riding your face." Korey couldn't believe the words leaving his lips. He'd been silent too long, craving what he never thought to have. Now Zeke watched him with lust in his gaze while offering Korey a life beyond anything he could've imagined. Korey planned to savor every second.

"Yes. Let's do that," Zeke said as he snatched Korey off his feet and headed for the bed. Unwanted nerves set in as he watched Zeke settle onto his back. "Get up here."

Korey licked his lips, fighting back the butterflies. The heat in Zeke's gaze was the only thing saving him from blushing and stammering his uncertainties. Instead, he held on to the headboard for support as he straddled Zeke's head. All nervousness fled as he stared down the line of his body. The hunger in Zeke's eyes was everything. The admission escaped with ease. "You're the sexiest man I've ever seen. I haven't looked away since the first time we met."

"I have things to say too, baby, but right now, I want this." Zeke licked Korey's erection from root to crown. The air left Korey's lungs on a *whoosh*. Then, the man took Korey down his throat, and time stopped. The world fell away. Nothing existed but the pull of Zeke's mouth and the tightening of his throat. Korey took what he offered, openly fucking the man's willing throat and mouth. He swore he could feel every taste bud as they scraped his crown.

Zeke moved from his dick to his balls, sucking them before licking Korey's asshole. Korey was sensation and desire. Nothing else. He was shameless. Moans filled the air. They had to be his, but Korey couldn't control the noises coming from his throat. His cock was back down Zeke's throat and Korey knew he wouldn't last much longer. His mind narrowed, focusing on nothing but his looming orgasm. He perched on the precipice. Korey rocked against Zeke's face, his control gone. He reached for release. The world tilted, and Korey found himself on his back. He didn't have time to come down from his high or cry out in denial over the loss of Zeke's mouth right at the moment he needed it most. Zeke ripped into a condom and was shoving his way inside Korey before he knew what happened. A cry tore from his lips. The most powerful orgasm he'd ever experienced slammed into him. Zeke's mouth covered his, swallowing his moans.

Zeke's dick stretched him wide and hit at all the right angles. Wave after wave of pleasure rocked Korey. Between Zeke's rough kiss and Korey's ecstasy, he couldn't catch his breath. He didn't care. Oxygen was overrated. Nothing mattered but Zeke's cock filling him and the mess between their bodies. Together, they were real and raw. Everything about them was perfect. Zeke pressed his forehead to Korey's. He sucked air through his open mouth, visibly fighting to breathe as he held Zeke's jaw. His eyes were shut. Korey couldn't look away. Zeke made being inside him look like it was the most amazing place on earth. Korey wanted to give him the world—make him scream. He wondered if Zeke owned toys. He'd love to suck the man's dick while pulling out some dildo moves. Fantasies of Zeke's cum coating his tongue and tying the man to the bed floated through Korey's mind.

"Come for me, sexy. I plan to spend the rest of my life rocking your world."

Zeke's eyes opened. He pumped faster while holding Korey's stare. The ecstasy made his eyelids heavy, but Korey couldn't close his eyes against this. His fingers dug into Zeke's back, urging him on. Sweat slickened their skin. Korey couldn't blink. He didn't want to miss Zeke's explosion. Zeke's muscles tensed. Korey held his breath. A loud gasp burst from Zeke. Korey swore he felt the moment their souls met.

Zeke collapsed into him, holding Korey tight enough he couldn't expand his lungs. "I took my pants off. You have to come home now," he said between loud breaths.

"Do you own handcuffs?"

A tired-sounding laugh brushed the shell of Korey's ear. "Do I need them to keep you from leaving me again?"

Korey stroked Zeke's back. "No. I was just thinking I'd like to keep you chained to the bed for a while when we get home. I'm not going anywhere, and I don't want you to either."

Zeke's lips brushed the spot beneath Korey's ear. "Don't worry. I'm in this forever," he whispered against Korey's skin.

Korey smiled against Zeke's shoulder. Every night he'd spent wishing Zeke was his had been worth it. "I can deal with forever," Korey whispered back, and he would. To be with Zeke, Korey would give anything. Do anything. Zeke meant everything to Korey. Always would.

Keep an eye out for Book 2, *Sugar Boss*.

ABOUT THE AUTHOR

Charity Parkerson is an award winning and multi-published author with several companies. Born with no filter from her brain to her mouth, she decided to take this odd quirk and insert it in her characters.

*Seven-time Readers' Favorite Award Winner
  *2015 Passionate Plume Award Finalist
  *2013 Reviewers' Choice Award Winner
  *2012 ARRA Finalist for Favorite Paranormal Romance
  *Five-time winner of The Mistress of the Darkpath

Connect with her online:

--Join my street team: facebook.com/TeamCharityParkerson
  --Sign up for my newsletter: http://bit.ly/CharityNews

--Website: charityparkerson.com

--Facebook:

facebook.com/authorCharityParkerson

facebook.com/TheMenofSin

--Twitter: twitter.com/CharityParkerso